W9-DJI-799

PETEY'S Bedtime Story

GAS

Beverly Cleary

PETEY'S Bedtime Story

Pictures by David Small

Morrow Junior Books New York

To my children

—B. C.

To Sarah

—D. S.

Pen, ink, and watercolors were used for the full-color artwork.
The text type is 13-point Cheltenham Book.

A different version of *Petey's Bedtime Story*
first appeared in *Wigwag* magazine, May 1990.

Text copyright © 1993 by Beverly Cleary
Illustrations copyright © 1993 by David Small
All rights reserved.
No part of this book may be reproduced or utilized
in any form or by any means, electronic or mechanical,
including photocopying, recording, or by any
information storage and retrieval system,
without permission in writing from the Publisher.
Inquiries should be addressed to
William Morrow and Company, Inc.,
1350 Avenue of the Americas, New York, NY 10019.

Printed in Hong Kong by South China Printing Company (1988) Ltd.

1 2 3 4 5 6 7 8 9 10

Library of Congress Cataloging-in-Publication Data
Cleary, Beverly. Petey's bedtime story / Beverly Cleary;
illustrated by David Small. p. cm.
Summary: During his usual bedtime routine, a young boy
comes up with his own version of the story about what happened
the day he was born.
ISBN 0-688-10660-9 (trade).—ISBN 0-688-10661-7 (library)
[1. Bedtime—Fiction. 2. Parent and child—Fiction.]
I. Small, David, 1945- ill. II. Title.
PZ7.C5792Pe 1993 [E]—dc20 92-6184 CIP AC

Some boys and girls don't like to go to bed, but Petey was not one of them. Petey liked to go to bed.

First came Petey's bath. His father scrubbed jam from his little boy's face, mud from his knees, and felt-tipped pen squiggles from his hands.

"Pow!" Petey slapped his hands down hard. Splashing water all over his father and the bathroom floor was fun.

"Silly kid," said Petey's father as he pulled him out of the tub. Petey stood first on one foot and then the other while his father dried him and stuffed him into his pajamas.

Petey ran into the living room crying, "Here I come, Mommy! Here I come!"

Petey's mother caught him, gave him a big hug, and said, "M-m-m. You are my sweet, clean little boy."

"Yes," agreed Petey, snuggling up to his mother. "Now read me a story." A story was always the next step in going to bed. So Petey's mother read a story about a baby alligator who went to sleep in nice soft mud. The story made her yawn.

Now it was Petey's father's turn. Petey chose his favorite book. With a sigh, Petey's father read Petey the story about four baby gophers falling asleep, all warm and cozy, in their soft little nest lined with grass. He yawned, too.

Petey did not yawn. After he studied every single picture in the book, he slid down from his father's lap and was off and running. "Catch me! Catch me!" he shouted.

Laughing, Petey's father chased Petey around the dining room one way while his mother chased him the other. Petey laughed hardest of all until he crawled under the dining room table. "You can't catch me!" he shouted.

"Oh, yes, I can!" Petey's father dragged him out by his feet and lifted him high above his head.

Petey held out his arms. "I'm an airplane!" he cried. "Make me fly!"

"I'll fly you right into your bed for the night," said Petey's father as he carried the airplane that used to be his little boy down the hall and dumped it on Petey's bed.

"There must be an easier way to get Petey to go to bed," said Petey's mother.

"If you find an easier way, let me know." Petey's father brought him a drink of water before he had time to ask.

"Don't forget to check for monsters," Petey said.

Petey's mother shut the closet door and looked under the bed. "No monsters hiding there," she told Petey.

Petey bounced off the bed. "Good night, Mr. Bunny," he said. "Good night, Papa Bear. Good night, piggy bank. Good night, Officer Robot. Daddy will buy you new batteries tomorrow."

"Now into bed with you," said Petey's father.

"But I haven't said my prayers." Petey knelt beside his bed and began, "God bless Mommy and Daddy," while his mother and father listened patiently because interrupting prayers was bad manners. Petey blessed everyone he could think of: his nursery school teachers, his aunts, uncles, cousins, the neighbors, and their dogs and cats. When Petey had blessed everyone in his nursery school, except those who threw sand, he gave up and climbed into bed. When his father turned off the overhead light, Petey said, "Good night, light bulb."

"*Now,*" said Petey. "Tell me the baby story." This was always the best part of going to bed.

"Oh, yes, the baby story. We can't forget the baby story." Petey's father made himself comfortable in a big chair while Petey's mother lay on the foot of the bed to listen.

"Once upon a time," Petey's father began, "two nice people were expecting a baby. They knew they had to go to the hospital when the baby was ready to arrive...." His head began to nod.

"Daddy, don't stop!" cried Petey. "Mommy's toenails come next. Don't leave out Mommy's red toenails."

Petey's father opened one eye. "Why don't you tell the story, Petey-boy? You must know it by heart."

"Okay," said Petey, and he began.

"One night Mommy painted her toenails so they would look pretty when she met the baby. After that, she was busy knitting a little blue sweater just the right size for..." Here Petey had a new thought. "Mommy, what was I wearing when I met you?" he asked.

"Hm-m?" Petey's mother lifted her head from the bedspread. "Oh. You were naked."

"Mommy!" Petey was shocked. His mother should have taken better care of him. Then he understood. She hadn't finished the sweater in time.

Petey continued his story, which, so far, was true. "Suddenly Mommy said, 'Quick. Our baby wants to meet us.' Daddy grabbed her suitcase and hurried her into the car. He drove off in the dark a hundred miles an hour."

"I did no such thing," said Petey's father.

"You do in my story," said Petey.

"If you say so," said Petey's father as he closed his eyes.

Petey decided to make the story more exciting. "Soon Mommy and Daddy heard a siren, *woo-oo woo-oo.* They saw red lights flashing on and off. Daddy said, 'Oh, no, not now!' and stopped the car.

"A police officer got out of his police car and said, 'Where do you think you're going?'

"Daddy said, 'To the hospital to meet our new baby. I don't have time to go to jail.'

"Mommy said, 'Please, Mr. Officer, I'll see that our baby's father behaves himself. If he doesn't, he can't watch TV for a whole week.'

“The officer said, ‘If you promise to make him mind, I won’t arrest him this time, but he better be good, or I’ll arrest him if I ever catch him again.’

“Daddy said, ‘Thank you, Mr. Officer. I promise to be good. Honest.’

“Then Daddy drove very, very slowly because he didn’t want to miss football on TV.

"Next, a big yellow fire engine came down the street going *ee-oo ee-oo*. Daddy pulled over to the curb.

"Mommy said, 'You can't stop now!'

"Daddy said, 'I have to, or I'll get arrested.' "

Petey had strayed so far from the story he had heard so many times that he now had to stop and think. What could happen next? "Oh, I know," said Petey. "Suddenly—the car stopped! Daddy forgot to buy gas.

" 'What do we do now?' asked Mommy. 'Our baby won't wait forever.'

"Daddy jumped out of the car and ran lickety-split to a gas station."

Here Petey was puzzled and asked, "Daddy, how can you buy gas without a car to put it in?"

"Hm-m?" Petey's father roused himself. "They lend you a can for the gas."

"Oh." Petey was satisfied. "Then Daddy ran faster than a rabbit back to the car, where Mommy was saying, 'Hurry, hurry!' Daddy poured the gas into the tank and drove off. 'Faster!' cried Mommy. 'Lots faster.'

"'I don't want the officer to catch me and make me miss TV,' said Daddy, but he did drive a tiny bit faster until he reached the hospital."

Petey was stumped. “Then what happened, Mommy?” he asked.

“When?” Petey’s mother did not even open her eyes.

Petey was impatient. “What happened when you got to the hospital?” His father always skipped that part.

“Oh.” Petey’s mother was barely awake. “Nurses came running and whisked me away in a wheelchair.”

Petey went on to make up his story. “A wheelchair. What fun! So Mommy got to race up and down while all the doctors and nurses shouted, ‘Here comes the baby! Here comes the baby!’ Mommy waved and blew kisses.

3A
←373-38

"Daddy yelled, 'Come on, baby! Come on!' the way he yelled at the TV set when he watched football.

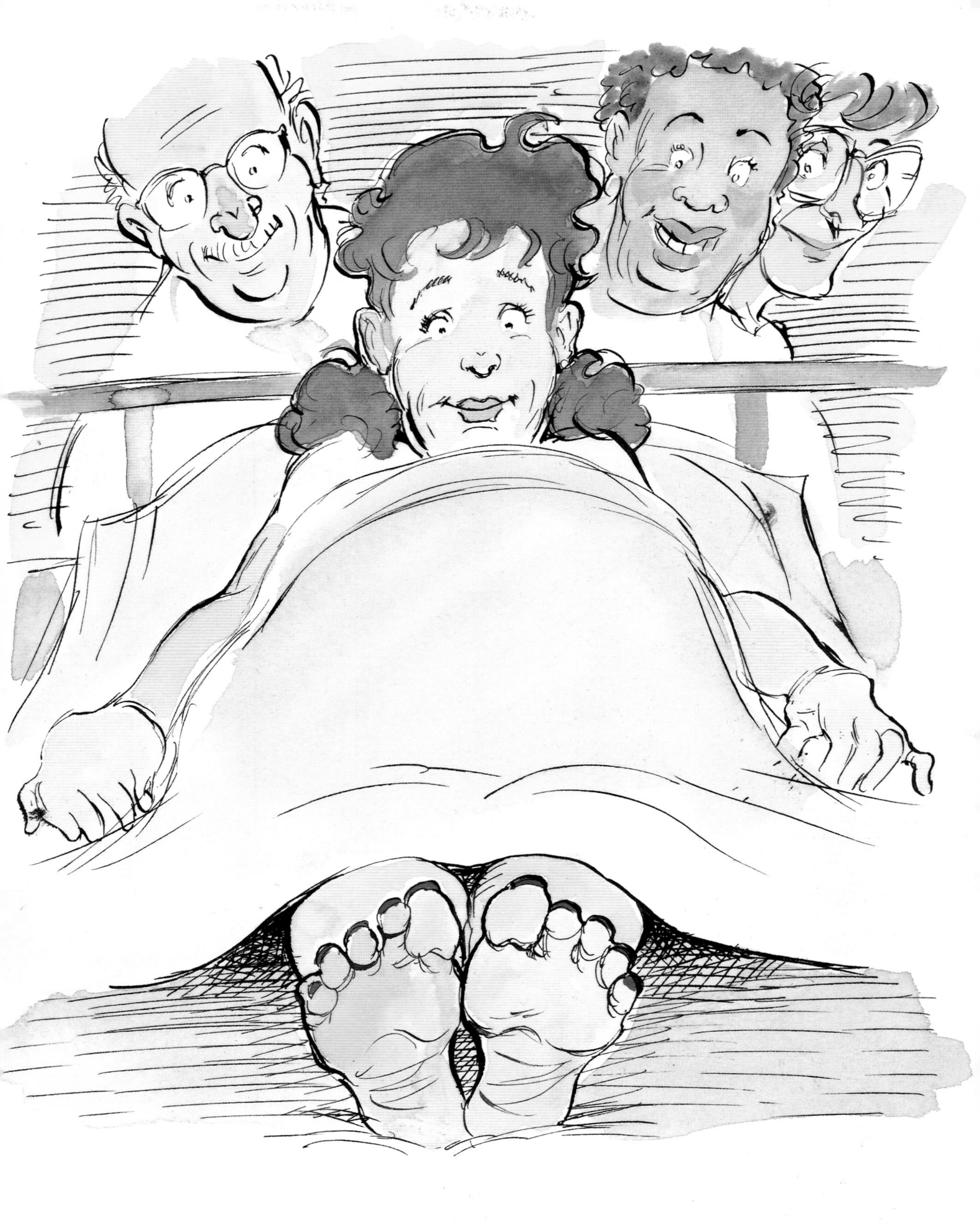

"Then the nurses pushed Mommy into a room where all the doctors and nurses looked at Mommy's pretty red toenails, and while they were looking—

"*Ta-da!*—the great baby, *me,* arrived. I was wearing a bow tie and cowboy boots."

Petey stopped to think. Babies, *other* babies, wore diapers, but of course he had never worn anything so babyish, so he added, "And my green coveralls.

“Everybody said, ‘What a great baby! He’s the greatest baby in the whole world.’

“Daddy said, ‘Yup, and I’m his father.’

“Mommy said, ‘I’m his mother. His name is Peter, but I’m going to call him Petey-boy.’

“Mommy was so happy and so sleepy she went to bed, but I ran up and down the hall telling everybody, ‘I’m a great baby! I am Petey-boy, a great baby!’

"By then it was morning. Daddy went out to move the car so he wouldn't get a parking ticket, but guess what? There was the policeman. 'Please, Mr. Policeman,' begged Daddy, 'don't give me a ticket. I don't want to miss TV. I couldn't move the car because we were so busy meeting our new baby.'

" 'Congratulations,' said the officer, 'but here's your ticket.'

“Daddy was very sad because he wanted to watch football, so he took the ticket to the city hall and said to the judge, ‘I didn’t mean to park so long, but I was waiting for our new baby. I promise to be good after this.’

“The judge said, ‘Sorry. You have to pay anyway.’ ”

Petey laughed and repeated, “ ‘Sorry. You have to pay anyway.’ ” These words were the words that ended the story every night. They were the best part of the story; his father really did get a parking ticket.

Petey discovered his mother and father were sound asleep. He slipped out of bed, kissed his parents gently so he wouldn't wake them, and pattered into the kitchen for a box of cookies,

which he carried into his parents' room.

He climbed into their big bed, where he ate every single cookie.

Then Petey lay back and listened to his father snore in the next room. He felt so warm, safe, full, and happy that he fell asleep all by himself in the grown-up bed full of crumbs. He didn't even need to look underneath the bed for monsters.